PIERCE FREELON

Daddy-Daughter Day

ILLUSTRATED BY
Olivia Duchess

Little, Brown and Company
New York Boston

ABOUT THIS BOOK

The illustrations for this book were done in Photoshop. This book was edited by Farrin Jacobs and designed by Sasha Illingworth. The production was supervised by Patricia Alvarado, and the production editor was Marisa Finkelstein. The text was set in Sofia Pro, and the display type is Bobby Jones.

 • Little, Brown and Company • Hachette Book Group 1290 Avenue of the Americas, New York, NY 10104 • Visit us at LBYR.com • First Edition: May 2022 • Little, Brown and Company is a division Hachette Book Group, Inc. • The Little, Brown name and logo are trademarks of Hachette Book Group, Inc. • The publisher is not responsible for websites (or their content) that are not owned by the publisher. • Library of Congress Cataloging-in-Publication Data Names: Freelon, Pierce, author. | Duchess, Olivia, illustrator. • Title: Daddy-daughter day / Pierce Freelon ; illustrated by Olivia Duchess. Description: First edition. | New York : Little, Brown and Company, 2022. | Audience: Ages 4–8 | Summary: In rhyming text, a father and daughter spend a day doing all kinds of things together. • Identifiers: LCCN 2021038948 | ISBN 9780316055260 (hardcover) • Subjects: CYAC: Stories in rhyme. | Fathers and daughters—Fiction. • Classification: LCC PZ8.3.F89 Dad 2022 | DDC [E]—dc23 • LC record available at https://lccn.loc.gov/2021038948 • ISBN 978-0-316-05526-0 • PRINTED IN THE UNITED STATES OF AMERICA • PHX • 10 9 8 7 6 5 4 3 2 1

For Stella. You are my shining star. —PF

To my mum (who doubled up as my dad). —OD

STELLA

By STELLA
6:59
KC

IT'S DADDY-DAUGHTER DAY!

Daddy, wake up!
We can't let this day go to waste.
Get out of bed or else...
this pillow is going in your face!

I’ll meet you in the kitchen for our daddy-daughter smoothie.
We could drink it on the sofa while we watch a morning movie,
then do our meditating, breathe in and breathe out,
clear our minds, so soothing.

What's it gonna be when I have you all to myself?
It's time to decide:
Go out in the world
or build a pillow fort and stay inside?

We can be lazy,
style our hair crazy.
Girls and dads only—
that's my favorite story.

WE'RE A DADDY-DAUGHTER POWER-COMBO SUPERHERO TEAM!

Girls and dads can rock in a heavy metal band
or frolic like two princesses when we play pretend
or travel far, like to another galaxy.
We are powered by the stars,
and we're stronger than gravity.

We both love adventures and science experiments.
I can be an astronaut or even an architect.
He can bake a cookie made out of chickpeas,
and I can go climbing and swing on a big tree.

My daddy is always fighting for progress.
We know everyone's rights should be respected.
I climb on Daddy's shoulders when we're down at the protest.
We help our neighbors out because our freedom is connected.
WE'RE A DADDY-DAUGHTER POWER-COMBO SUPERHERO TEAM!

UNITY
LOVE EACH OTHER
LOVE IS LOVE
WORLD PEACE
WE STAND TOGETHER

Time for hopscotch!
Of course he brought chalk.
Seems like Daddy stops to talk
with every parent on the block!

Should we shoot hoops?
I'm ready to play.
I'll flush the alley-oop!

Then host a half-court tea party in the middle of the day.

DADDY-DAUGHTER
DINNER DEAL
I owe you dinner
i o u clean dishes

Heading home, we make a deal.
If I do the dishes, then Daddy cooks the meal.
When Mama asks how our day went,
I laugh and tell her Daddy's my favorite.

Sun is going down now,
I get into my jammies.

First we read a book,
then we perform a bedtime concert for my grammy.

Close your eyes, Daddy says, it's sleepy time.
Tomorrow we're gonna press rewind!
Dream sweet, my star, creative, wise, and brave.

Get ready for another
POWER-COMBO SUPERHERO DADDY-DAUGHTER DAY!

6:59